THE STUFF OF MONUMENTS

THE STUFF OF MONUMENTS

A Collection of Short Stories

RICHARD A. CROUSEY

LITTLE THINGS

"Little" things occur regularly, forbidding us to recognize their significance. What ultimately causes them to blossom into sweetness is their fading away.

"Little" things go quietly without fanfare, yet they are the substance of life.

The seasons of our lives are made up of the "stuff" that went before. Nothing is truly lost. As one picture begins to fade, another begins to dawn.

CONTENTS

PREFACE

So what kind of stuff *are* monuments made of? Being American, the mention of monuments brings to mind the Lincoln Memorial, the Washington Monument or Mount Rushmore. Therefore, the obvious answer is stone. You may remember in the Old Testament God commands the Israelites to build monuments on various occasions. Remember the pile of stones [one for each tribe] accumulated at the Jordon River after crossing into the Holy Land from their exile in Egypt? God expects monuments to remind us of something that has happened before which is worth commemorating. This is true in our American examples, as well, but what purpose is served by this? What is the point? Simply, it is hard to know where you are going if you don't remember where you have been. Remembering the sacrifices of others should make us grateful for what we have and enlighten us on how those before us contributed to our blessings of today.

In a spiritual sense, we can sometimes look back to see where the monuments in our lives have been laid. These will be places that God has touched us and we were moving in the right direction [toward Him]. When storm clouds loom ahead, we then have the opportunity to look backwards at our monuments and determine the direction we need to head even as the storms or fog move in. The problem tends to be that people do not often erect monuments for themselves. God moves in a glorious way in our life and we are truly grateful and may even take the time to say thanks, but we continue with life without further notice. How foolish. Remembering these times gives us strength and faith for the present and the future. The reality is, we cannot remember events without memorials to give witness to them.

CENTERFIELD

Caleb is one of four children, eldest of three sons. He has always loved baseball. Centerfield is his position, always was. Now graduated from Messiah College, he played baseball for fifteen years. His coach repeatedly told us, "Caleb plays centerfield like the morning dew, he's all over." His senior season, Cale led his team in four offensive categories including a batting average of .388. The story centers on his last game.

My wife and I had driven three hours east to see our son's final baseball game. We had missed more college games than we had seen but this one required our attendance and was certain to be bittersweet.

The contest started like most but a peculiar suspense building. By the fifth inning I was driven to take a short walk. Game noises disappeared as I wandered on. I needed a moment with God. What to say? Thoughts ran desperately through my mind, congealing in a lucid moment. This game, my son, the experience are each important to me but why so exaggerated now? I always loved watching Cale play ball, somehow though I had missed the immensity of the blessing. It was the disappearing, even as I walked that somehow gave it value. We've experienced similar moments with each child; Cambric's wedding, Josh's last soccer game and Rod starting grade school. It's the disappearing that catches our attention. I spoke with the Lord attempting to express thanks, but mostly I was silent. Finally, I worked my way back to the field where Cale's final at bat was a double.

Following the game, Caleb shared his own experience.

While going onto the outfield (mid-game), he found himself disengaged from the game. Realizing what was fading before him, Cale looked around the field, the stands, the people he had grown to love. Countless times he had stood at "his" spot in centerfield. This time, with misty eyes, he witnessed his surroundings for what seemed the first time.

Our experiences were different but mirrored one another. I sense God was helping us see more clearly what had previously been taken for granted. "Little" things occur regularly, forbidding us to recognize their significance. What ultimately causes them to blossom into sweetness is the fading away. I suspect all of life may be like this. "Little" things go quietly without fanfare, yet they are the substance of life. When did my children last run out to welcome me home by hanging on my legs? When was the last time Cale closely followed my every step with his blue, plastic lawnmower? When did I last go into each bedroom to pray with them before a night's sleep? When did I last complain about Josh or Rod asking too many questions? The first day of school and graduations mark time but what about the multitude of days in between? When was the last time I heard Cambric's soft voice down the hallway and never gave it a second thought?

The seasons of our lives surely change. On a positive note, they are made up of the "stuff" that went before. Nothing is truly lost. As one picture begins to fade, another begins to dawn. "For now we see through a glass darkly; but then face to face; now I know in part, but then shall I know even as also I am known." The fabric of each life is unique, finely woven of insignificant threads.

Surprisingly the Falcons made the playoffs and "now for the rest of the story." Warm-up included a demonstration of "shadow ball" (confusing novice fans). I spent most of the game on a grassy terrace adjacent to right field. It provided a great vantage and a place alone. A well-played game ensued but not to our favor. From my private box I watched my son sit down on the grass to remove his spikes. He had played ball for fifteen years and now at the pinnacle of his game, it was over. I tried convincing myself that I understood his thoughts. Truthfully, I could not know. His thoughts would remain his. I did know my thoughts for I too had earned an experience all my own. We met, cautiously giving each other a hug. I invited him to my terrace, showing him the woodpecker's nest and butternut tree…anything to avoid the subject at-hand. Finally I tried thanking him for all those wonderful moments. My voice cracked as tears washed my cheeks. With labored effort Caleb spoke saying there was no one he'd rather have in the stands.

These threads crossing the shuttle may be insignificant to some but not to me. There is a popular song today, "Put me in coach, I'm ready to play today…I know I can be centerfield." How apt for my son? Now he is at his best, ready to play but the season is over. Perhaps a lifetime has positioned me to be the best father I can be, strange now that the season is drawing to a close. Rod is playing a baseball game tomorrow at home. You bet I'll be there.

Richard A. Crousey 2001

ENDURING FRIENDSHIPS

Friendships are difficult to understand. Why do we consider some people friends and others do not qualify? What is an enduring friend? For purposes here I will be inclined to say that an enduring friend is also a best friend but a giant step beyond. "Best friends" in my experience are not as rare and imply a temporal relationship. Perhaps, if you experience three enduring friendships in a lifetime, you are blessed. If you think you've had 10 over your lifetime, my fear is you may have had none. Let's try to make sense of just what allows an enduring friendship to occur.

Are friends about similarities? This would seem reasonable. We should like the people we have the most in common with. Certainly this plays a role but is it the answer? I remember being proud of my children as they were growing up. Mostly I was proud of their behavior, their thoughts and the way they showed love. It was good to see them turning out well and getting along well together. Then there were those moments when each of them could anger me by their behavior, words, etc. Here's the rub. When I would try to analyze what displeased me, I frequently came up with an uncomfortable result. So often the source of this displeasure pointed directly at me. You know the old adage, "Don't do as I do, do as I say." Yes, on many occasions I could see my children following footsteps of mine they would have been well to avoid; strange since they were behaving like me. The same is true about other people we meet. Sometimes if we take a moment to analyze the situation, we are most uncomfortable when they remind us of ourselves. This may seem a paradox but true none the less. Enduring friendships do not revolve around similarities.

Is it about physical appearance? Surely some people are more attractive than others by virtue of their appearance. Some women are attractive without doing anything in particular…it doesn't involve their wardrobe or make-up. They are just naturally attractive. Other women are very good at applying make-up well and dressing stylishly. (My strong preference remains with the first camp). Yes, I hear you saying, "It's not about the outside, it's about the inside." You're right of course; things like character, compassion, morals, faith, hopefulness, joy, patience, etc. are not visible from the outside and are surely more important. It takes time to find these qualities and more time to have them put to the test. Seeing them placed in a smelter and the dross burned off and finding them pure & true…this is a critical element to enduring friendships.

Is it about sharing philosophies? How nice when people get together and talk about issues they agree on. Things flow well but you can only go so far with this. Truly fascinating people challenge us. This can be done without disagreeing; they just force one to think a little deeper into a subject and are willing to question what may at first appear obvious. Our home was a Christian home…not perfect but well intended. Our children were always encouraged to question their faith and they proved more than able to do so. A faith that cannot stand up to legitimate questions is not worth much and will have a hard time standing up to the tests of a lifetime. Unfortunately, this questioning may be misinterpreted; but never by an enduring friend. My Christianity is critical to me yet many of my friends are not Christian. This alone does not inspire an enduring friendship. Many times I have wished my skills in sharing the good news were better so I could be more effective in reaching out, then I remember the Holy Spirit is the one responsible and all I have to do is be obedient in sharing as He leads.

Is there something to the "chemistry" of a friendship? My best friend is surely my wife. We certainly had/have chemistry but that does not a friendship make. At first this sounds promising and perhaps it is a contributor but not an answer in its own right. Keep in mind the number of people who get married after falling in love. If *falling in love* is a reason for marriage then *falling out of love* is just as easy. With chemistry still in mind, I did not fall in love with Marilyn; I *chose* to love her and *chose* to make an oath to God accordingly. One might say, the door in, is the door out. For me to no longer love my wife, I would have to *choose* not to love her and in the same sense I would have to *choose* to break my vow to God. In a similar way we choose a good friendship.

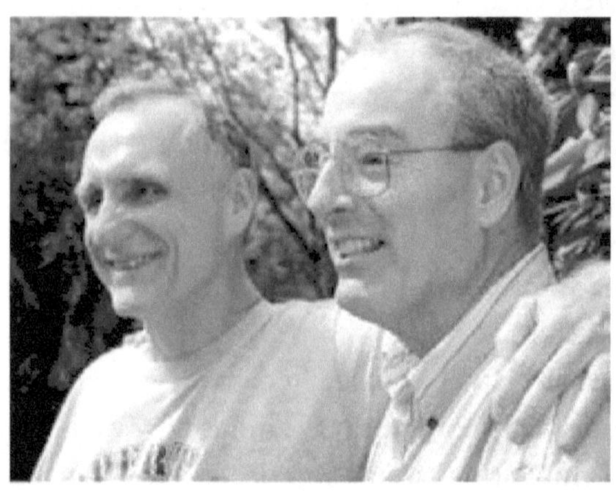

It will not fall apart because we have a disagreement. It will survive a lengthy absence. A good friendship will stand up to the tests of time and hardship.

On a personal note, I grew up in Pennsylvania and participated as a member of a good high school wrestling team. Naturally, I spent many hours with team mates I considered to be good friends. Do I still have a relationship with any of these people? No, I have virtually no knowledge of them. A year or so ago I contacted my old wrestling coach and it was a joy to speak with him. I was shocked at how good his memory was as he referred to me as that towheaded boy with a lot of heart and a marginal skill level. Coach also remembered that we had gone undefeated my senior year. Enduring friends however: 0. So, with all of those years invested there were no on-going contacts/ friendships except for family. Moving on, I attended Grove City College for four years, a great experience with terrific friendships. Were there any enduring friendships? Yes, finally one such friendship[1] entered my life. Was there something unique to single out this experience? No, not that I remember. It was a normal meeting. We shared classes since we both were engineering majors. Jim was from Ohio. A contributing element was that Jim and I were roommates for our last three years at college. Surely, we were both friends with many others including a third roommate for the same period of time but none of these friendships endured except ours. Did we know then that something very special had occurred? I don't think so. You see at this age, opportunities occur in rapid succession and one is inclined to believe similar experiences will continue throughout life. The uniqueness of opportunities and experiences come & go with inadequate notice or appreciation. Jim now lives in San Antonio, TX. He served 20 years in the Army and received his retirement. I worked exclusively in the steel industry as an engineer and Jim (although graduating as an engineer), worked in physical rehabilitation. Jim had two sisters and I had one. My wife and I went on to have four children under our roof and Jim had a short marriage without children. Our lives went in directions nearly as diverse as possible. We sometimes went years without communicating, yet when we talk it is as though time has stopped, waiting for us to speak again. This relationship to time I do believe is a critical element in identifying an enduring relationship but is not of much help in understanding how they form.

As I already mentioned, my wife is my best friend.[2] Using the triune nature of God as a template for man, (mind, spirit and body); Marilyn and I share intimacy at each of these levels. Jim and I walk in a much more limited sphere. There are other very good friends in my life (some enduring) but discussing these two is adequate for the purpose. The point stands made that describing a relationship like this is difficult even without an effort to understand its origin.

Contributing factors of an enduring friendship include the following thoughts.

Personal similarities can both help or inhibit such a friendship.

The character of the individuals is essential. This includes those hidden qualities that are instrumental in defining who we are. Words to consider are compassion, faith, hope, love, kindness, legitimate concern for the other, morals, etc. These may be open to debate but never off the table.

No matter how many characteristics we share; they must stand up to questioning, time (durations apart as well as long spells together), disappointment and trials (body, soul & spirit) all without damaging the relationship and with each party slow to pass judgment.[3]

One sure key element is respecting the other's opinions enough to listen.[4] This is not as easy as it sounds. We can commit to hear someone out without acknowledging their ability to share something of value.

Count your enduring friendships. How many have you experienced? Please recognize their rarity and acknowledge the crucial part they play in your life and the rare blessing each represents.

[1] "…there is a friend that sticketh closer than a brother."
Proverbs 18:24 KJV

[2] "Behold, thou art fair, my love; behold, thou art fair; thou hast doves' eyes. Behold, thou art fair, my beloved, yea, pleasant: also our bed is green." ("Briar Patch" green)
Solomon's Song 2:15-16 KJV

[3] "Faithful are the wounds of a friend..." Proverbs 27:6 KJV

[4] "Iron sharpeneth iron; so a man sharpeneth the countenance of his friend."
Proverbs 27:17 KJV

Richard Crousey April, 2009

FRIENDLY SOUNDS

One recent night I awoke to a pleasant, sweet-smelling breeze. Early summer blossoms combined with the fragrance of a light rain caused me to take notice. I took intentional deep breaths comforted by the softness of the night. My senses were heightened and I was now fully awake. In the distance, I recognized immediately a repetitive, soothing sound. It was steel moving across the dies of a forging press at a local steel making facility. It was a pleasant sound that complimented the night. Shortly, there was the sound of a distant train. It too had a voice speaking sweetly to the early morning. Questions came to my mind but the night with its caressing sounds lulled me back to a deep sleep.

In the morning, the experience of the night with its accompanying questions returned. What causes a sound to be friendly? One might expect a factory sound to be an intrusion to a quiet night; likewise the train. Surely those living in close proximity to the sounds might refer to them as an unwelcome intrusion, but there is more to the equation than the intensity of the sounds.

For years I have loved canoeing on local rivers. It is great to experience the scenes and solitude of remote sections of the Conemaugh, Kiskiminitas and Youghiogheny Rivers.

Noteworthy to our original questions, rivers are routinely used as train right-of-ways. Since I so enjoy the quiet of the river, you might expect the sound of an oncoming, nearby train to be an unwelcome intruder. To the contrary, the train briefly interupts the scene but in a nice way. The train belongs to the river. Should I hear car traffic or an overhead plane, these are perceived as negative interruptions to the river environ.

What makes the difference -how universal are my perceptions?

I confess I come to the question with my own personal biases. My grandfather worked for the Pennsylvania Railroad and always spoke well of his job. To hear him, you would think he owned the railroad. He would routinely speak saying, "We own all of this property over here;" or "Our passenger schedule through Pitcairn is changing tomorrow." How may he have influenced my impressions? My family's original home & my first memories arise from the town of Homestead, Pennsylvania. Homestead once had the largest steel-making facility in the world. The factory was profitable and active in my youth. Some might say the sounds, the smells the pervasive dirt were unnatural, unwanted pollutants. Not so to the people of Homestead. These "pollutants" were the sounds and smells of prosperity and considered intimate friends. Everyone recognized the slamming of rails into the bite of the rolling mills and the "aroma" arising from the open hearth furnaces. We also recognized the powerful crunch of steam hammers or presses forging the steel to a new shape. Later my children grew up in Latrobe, Pa.

and I worked for the local steel mill where the Mesta Press forged steel within earshot of our bedroom window. Steel crossing the dies displayed a familiar, comfortable rhythm to me.

Do these thoughts respond to the question? It's obvious I come well-equipped with biases. Do others enjoy the distant track clatter and engines and whistles of the railroad? I personally love to fly (the smaller the plane the better), and I find yet the roar of their engines an intrusion to nature. I confess there is a noticeable deep drone to the engines of WWII vintage aircraft which I do find pleasant. I rode motorcycles for years as a young man and still their engine roar is an obnoxious interference to the calmness of any night.

How about the sounds appearing in nature? Spring "peepers" (small frogs), announce the coming of a new season. These peep their consistent songs all night, only interrupted by the appearance of intruders, which bring an instant silence. How differently the birds chant their intimate songs of spring? It is especially delightful as they bring on the early morning daylight. Then there are the late summer mouthpieces of insects; crickets, katydids & locusts each having their own part in a nighttime symphony. As autumn approaches, all the more carefully I listen to the music before it disappears with the first frost. Who can resist the synchronous pulses of ocean waves or the repetitious gurgling of a woodland brook?

Perhaps the commonality of friendly sounds is found in the way that some of man's creations imitate the patterns and pitches of nature. I cannot be sure. I have done no surveys nor do I intend to do so. What others think will not bias my opinions. This to be sure, religiously I await the announcement of spring and the chatter of autumn insects. Paths will continue to lead me back to the river with its entertaining cedar waxwings, an occasional eagle and the harmonious drone of a coming locomotive.

Richard Crousey June 28th, 2007

LIGHT & DARKNESS

It is frequently said that talk is cheap. It is easy to speak about situations you don't have to experience. Outside observation can only go so far; as the adage says, "Walk a mile in my shoes."

Light is the condition where you can see what is around you. Darkness then means the absence of light and is a condition where we must depend on senses other than our eyes. Darkness seems to be the natural condition of the universe and this darkness must be driven away by light.

Scripturally, Jesus tells us that He is the "Light of the World."[1] Note the implication then that darkness is the natural state of the world. Another piece of critical information is that Jesus, during his trial, informed Pilot that He "had come to bear witness to the Truth."[2] Pilot mockingly responded, "And what is truth?" The Father of truth is God while the father of lies is Satan. Keep in mind that Satan always tries to place himself on the same level as God. Likewise, Jesus is both light and truth incarnate while Satan is all about darkness and deception.

Here we find ourselves living in a world misled by Satan from birth. As we mature, the "hound of Heaven" begins to track us down so we can come to the knowledge of the truth. C. S. Lewis (himself run down by the hound of Heaven), comments that if you want to remain an atheist, "...you must be very careful what you read."

Let us look at the dilemma just described. The world is about darkness, yet it appears to be well lit by the sun. Notice during the day people find it easier to do many chores like driving, walking, gardening, etc. At night people begin to sense fear due to the limitation of their vision. Night is not so much about what you cannot see as it is about what you can imagine. So darkness brings on fear even when there is no justification for it. If the world is in darkness why does it appear to be so well lit? Did you ever wonder about the monumental lighting displays in Times Square or Las Vegas (areas of distinct darkness yet well lit with artificial light)? Appropriate if Satan is deceiving us about what truth is. Much of what we consider darkness (lumens or lack of morals), occurs after nightfall. People may fear darkness but they also hope to use darkness to hide. It seems like a natural cover for those things appearing ugly in the light of day.

What does this mean to a Christian? We want to seek God's truth and we want Jesus to live within us and we want His light to shine from us.[3] Let me pose a question. If I had a flashlight on a sunny day it would attract no attention at all, right? Others could not even tell whether it was lit. Are the batteries good? Is the bulb burnt out? Is the switch working? So then with the light of a Christian; we all want to be in the light and yet we want our light to shine for others to see the joy of Christ within us. You can see the contradiction here; light best shows to be shining when it is surrounded by darkness. No one of the light enjoys the darkness but it is in darkness we can best show the world what we have at the center of our lives. The temptation is to be fearful when darkness falls, and it will, by the order of all of nature. In reality darkness presents us with an opportunity. Hopefully, we have nothing we want to hide in the darkness. Instead we want to share our light. We really don't have much to offer when goodness, health & light are all around us. The evidence backing up our words is to be the light shining in the darkness. This must make the Christian different or, God forbid, prove talk is cheap.

[1] "…his life gave light to everyone…" John 1:4 CEV

[2] "…To this end I was born, and for this cause came I into the world, that I should bear witness unto the truth. Everyone that is of the truth heareth my voice."
St. John 18:37 KJV

[3] "The light has come into the world, and people who do evil things are judged guilty because they love the dark more than the light. People who do evil hate the light and won't come to the light, because it clearly shows what they have done. But everyone who lives by the truth will come to the light, because they want others to know that God is really the one doing what they do."
John 3:19-21 CEV

Richard A. Crousey April, 2009

OUR BRIAR PATCH

Allow me to relate a memory from childhood. My sister, Karen, & I heard tales as told by "Uncle Remus," from a book so entitled. I understand the book is somewhat difficult to find today, likely due to the imaginations of "political correctness." You see, Uncle Remus was a black man with very colloquial speech. Personally, I see no shame in this. He lacked a formal education but was wise with a strong moral compass as portrayed in the stories, definitely someone deserving an ear.[1]

Please forgive any errors as I attempt to remember characters from this book as related to the story of "Tar Baby." You must first recognize the three characters. First is Br'er (brother) Rabbit, quick afoot and of mind and as appropriate for a rabbit, always on the run trying to avoid capture. Not well suited as the moral protagonist of the narrative since he displays serious character flaws. The second character is Br'er Fox, a wily chap as you might expect with singleness of mind concerning the capture of Br'er Rabbit. Lastly, we find a co-conspirator called Br'er Bear, large and slow afoot and of mind…the antithesis of Br'er Rabbit. The one thing the two shared in common was their willingness to be led astray…Br'er Rabbit by his own contrivance and Br'er Bear by the influence of questionable company.

Now to my recollection of the story: Br'er Fox had used the hot temper of Br'er Rabbit to capture him using a "baby" formed of tar and dressed like a child. The rabbit became stuck in the tar as he tried to teach Tar Baby a lesson for not acknowledging him. The more he kicked

& hit Tar Baby the more he became stuck, which led to his capture. At last Br'er Fox and Br'er Bear have Br'er Rabbit in their clutches, now what to do with him? They discussed various options observing Br'er Rabbit (to see what would trouble him the most). Br'er Rabbit responds, "Please don't throw me in the briar patch." Well, if that is Br'er Rabbit's greatest fear then that was just the thing to do. Br'er Rabbit was picked up and indignantly flung into the briar patch. Br'er Fox and Br'er Bear waited listening for screams but heard none. What had happened? Finally, Br'er Rabbit began laughing incessantly and yelled out from the patch saying he had been born in this briar patch and it was both home and protection to him. So once again Br'er Fox and Br'er Bear had been foiled by Br'er Rabbit.

So why do I relate this childhood memory? My wife and I recently discovered we shared a briar patch of our own. You see, I had become very ill with doctors saying I would not live long. What an awful place to find ourselves with thorns all around.

These thorns caused stinging pain as we fought against our circumstances. I was educated to take control of events and gain an upper-hand with appropriate action. I also had a lifetime practicing this craft on my job. On this occasion, I had no secular response available to me and fell victim to the stress it caused. I was a control-freak sadly out of control.

God and I shared some serious conversations. Immediately, prior to my first surgery and diagnosis I felt certain God had provided some direction as to where my life was heading. I was to continue teaching an adult men's Sunday school class. My wife and I were to host another foreign exchange student. I was to do some writing and Marilyn and I were to host a small group Bible study. This sickness was unlikely to provide either the time or energy to accomplish these goals. What then had gone wrong? Had I misunderstood my Father? I remember coming to the conclusion that God had either caused this illness or He had allowed it and from my point of view there was precious little difference. I have since heard this more artfully stated as, "Nothing attends a Christian without it first filtering through the hands of God." So what is an out of control control-freak to do?

The first miracle I remember came in the form of direction. I was contacted by a couple of family members and then by an old college friend, 1000 miles away, and also by a friend at work. Each of them offered something a little different; a doctor's name, a hospital, a type of surgery. With little effort it was clear that all of these pointed in exactly the same direction with the doctor, surgery and hospital all potentially available just 50 miles from home. These pieces fell gloriously together with virtually no effort from me and we proceeded accordingly. In time, I also came to acknowledge that I enjoyed tremendous support groups surrounding me in various ways. My wife had always been the most compassionate person I had ever met (even to a fault) and now I was the key beneficiary of her compassion. My children and family, always a blessing, came once again to the forefront of my benefactors. There were huge Christian circles praying for me when it was nearly impossible to pray for myself. So both my home Church and numerous others reached up to God on my behalf. Additionally, my employer and those I worked with were most understanding throughout the process. And friends, what wonderful things can I say about them with their continual offering of love and support. You know who you are and I thank all of you ever so much. These all represent miracles.

I will not deceive...the going was very tough and at one moment I felt abandoned by God but, as I hope you know, feelings are not to be trusted. They can lie. As I look back, even at that very dark moment, I was encircled by some of God's saints who showed me great compassion and love.

Let's fast forward, there were two three-month chemotherapy sessions and two difficult surgeries (the second being especially hard with a three week hospital stay). Today it is two years after the diagnosis (that offered me 12-18 months to live). This week I have another CT scan which I am secure will provide another good report. I continue teaching the Men's Sunday School class. I did some writing, much of it while receiving chemo. We have a another foreign exchange student living with us and my wife and I have participated in small group Bible studies at our church and remain secure in thinking we will host more studies in our home.

So what then about the Briar Patch? This has truly been a thorny battle while suffering many scratches and bruises. Well into the process, my wife, Marilyn, and I discovered we did not have to fight the thorns. We could hunker down together at their base and the thorns helped protect us in peculiar ways. In our briar patch there are no needles, knives, chemo nor even other people. There may be needles in the morning or on the following day but not while we are in our patch. We found we could even travel paths unrecognized by others and lie down comfortably in each others arms knowing the seeds for the thorns had filtered through the fingers of God. We cannot live in the Briar Patch; we must come out at times for life to continue but how sweet to know we can find peace together in this place, our own personal Briar Patch as we strive toward Paul's admonition:

"...I have learned to be content whatever the circumstances." Phil 4:11

March, 2009 Richard Crousey

[1] This same injustice is done as schools have seemingly removed Samuel Clemens' "Huckleberry Finn" from study, again for political correctness. What a sham when you consider that "Jim" is the character most admired by Huck and Huck's only genuine protector. Jim walks well above other characters as he struggles to restore his own family,

while legitimately caring about those around him even at his own personal expense; surely a man to be admired.

Addendum:

OK you heard the story as best I could tell it. Now there is more to the story. Things have not gone as prayed for or hoped for. The surgeon gave us his interpretation of the most recent CT scan and it was not encouraging. He believes there's evidence of two more areas with cancer. He cannot see the tumors but he believes he can see the results of them. One area is a lung with a fluid build-up and the other area is a blockage forming at my bile duct. The surgeon believes this to be an inoperable condition but as he said he has sometimes been wrong. What this means is that I have had a couple more tests this week, an appointment to see another doctor on Tuesday next week and another medical test/procedure on Wednesday following this appointment. No one has firmed a strategy yet, simply not enough information to go on. Receiving the news was a kick in the gut but as we were leaving I looked at Marilyn and said, "We were in God's hands when we walked into the hospital and we remain in God's hands as we leave." What better place to find myself but in the hands of the Great Physician.

STANDING OVATION

Growing up in the early 50's, nearly every father in our neighborhood was involved in WWII in one way or another. My father was one of them, having served as a Marine in the South Pacific. As a child he was just a great dad. As I aged and read books and saw movies on the subject, my appreciation for Dad's participation in The War flourished. I remember vividly when my eldest son turned nineteen. Dad had turned nineteen with Guadalcanal facing him and it was beyond my imagination that he was such a tender age in this conflict.

Dad rarely spoke of the war. When direct questions were asked, one could draw from him only the barest of responses. I was seriously interested in Dad's experiences but it was clear this was a place I could never go. Dad belonged to a fraternity with an elite membership and I could not trespass there.

Let me share an experience that tenderly touched my heart. I was now in grade school and accompanying Dad on any trip was considered a great event. One day we went together to buy tires for our car. After some time we finally arrived at Kroll Brothers Tire Shop on the North Side of Pittsburgh. I was curious why we passed other tire shops on our way and inquired why we had traveled so far. Dad spoke openly on this occasion telling me his best friend in the Marines was Harry Kroll. Harry had been killed early in the war. This was a rare moment to hear Dad speak of his lost friend. Dad, of course, was honoring his friend with this regular pilgrimage. Following Guadalcanal, Dad had gone on to fight in Bougainville, Iwo Jima and Guam. He never willingly spoke of these places or events. On one occasion I read to my father a short piece I had found about a valiant group of Marines who were indispensable in the early fighting on Bougainville. The piece had been written by a high ranking officer. I was strongly suspicious that Dad had participated in this action. As I read how the officer described the event and marveled at the young men who had accomplished what seemed to be impossible (due to heavy enemy fire and thick jungle conditions), Dad listened attentively. The officer went on to express his praise and thanks for the efforts of the young Marines and for their courage under fire. Dad offered no response but I a tear drifted down his cheek.

This past 4th of July, my family attended our town's local parade. I was pleased to see that all of the soldiers received a standing ovation from the crowd. Dad, please accept these words as a standing ovation from your grateful son.

Veteran: Charles Crousey USMC 3rd Division
WWII action: Guadalcanal, Bougainville, Guam, Iwo Jima
233 East Patty Lane, Monroeville, PA 15146
Story written by: Richard Crousey (son)
Latrobe, PA 15650

Richard A. Crousey
July 8, 2007

THE QUAD

As a young man, God regularly tried to get my attention. On a couple of occasions words of a poem would form in my mind. Most commonly this occurred while driving. The words came so rapidly I had to pull off the road to write them down. Although I am no poet, the poems read well.

I did record these poems and managed to keep track of them for years but ultimately I misplaced them. Shame on me, since I truly believe they were a gift from God. The only words I remember are the ending of one poem and read as follows: "Peace, peace when there is no peace. One hope eternal lies veiled by human tears. Sweet little Jesus boy we don't know who you are." These words were burned deeply into my mind. I suspect I thought these communications would continue but they did not and I repent my cavalier, youthful attitude. God also spoke occasionally through dreams. I rarely remember dreams but these were unique, clear in my mind come morning. I am now able to recall only one such dream. Grant me a moment to provide a short background to help you understand the dream.

I attended Grove City College in Pennsylvania. These were very good years for me. I appreciated the education I received and the friendships that developed although, only one such friendship has endured the 37 years since graduation. (Jim is a subject for another day). Our well-groomed campus was beautiful and I frequently took walks alone past manicured lawns and through groves of old forest trees. One notable feature was a large grass expanse in the center of campus. This area was called "the Quad." Now allow me to share the dream.

It was a gorgeous, sunny day with a dark blue sky and soft white clouds. I was sitting on the warm, grassy Quad and found myself wrestling with a lion cub (much as you would play with a puppy). I was enjoying this thoroughly and all felt right with the world. Quite unexpectedly, the cub caught its leg in an awkward fashion, yelping in pain.

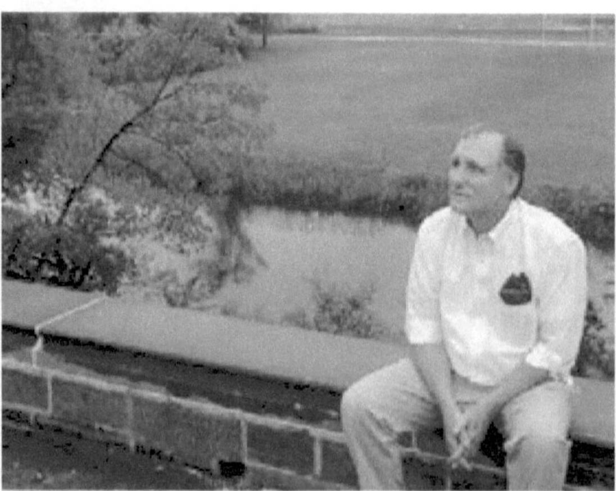

It proved to be a compound fracture with the cub in serious pain, unable to walk. Despite the clear sky, all had turned dark in my mind.

Both the cub and I were now in distress. From somewhere I received the instruction to take a knife (which appeared conveniently), and thrust it into the heart of the lion cub, presumably to end its suffering. Reluctantly, I did as instructed. The cub died instantly. For me the world had turned black. In agony I pondered how all could be so pleasurable one moment while so quickly turning all wrong. Suddenly I received a new command to remove the knife from the lion cub's body and again I obediently responded. As the knife exited the wound, instantly the cub was alive and well without a broken leg. The lion was again drawing me to an unspeakable joy and wanted to resume play, which we did. Again the dream had turned on a dime and all was well again with my world. I believe the new-felt joy was even heightened by the earlier distress.

Come morning, the dream remained crystal clear and weighed heavily on my spirit. Now I had to come up with an interpretation. I never sought outside help for this and over time came to the following interpretation.

First I recognized that at no time during the dream did I have any personal control over the situation. The dream played through with me as a participant who only responded to commands (that appeared to make no sense). I have come to see the lion cub as a representation of my soul. The broken leg was destruction that sin had brought into my life with no apparent cure available. The command to kill the cub represents a call to place my soul on the altar of sacrifice. By doing so, my selfish desire to be in control of my life (broken beyond repair), was now gone. The knife being withdrawn was Jesus' response to the surrender and He provided a new life free from the broken leg of sin. The new life, however, was no longer my own. It still was filled with joy & skies remained clear but the joy was at a new higher level.

This is the dream with the interpretation I have come to accept. Did I follow through with the dream and place my life on the altar? No, I cannot say that I did. I suspect I placed some carefully selected parts of my life there while hanging on to control of areas too difficult to part with. The dream, however, makes it clear that all must be placed on the altar. So what have I done? Am I so foolish as to slowly, painfully insert the blade ever deeper and with such reluctance? It seems so.

At the beginning of this year, life was looking very good. I suspect I was more obedient to God this past year then I have ever been. The relationship with Marilyn (my wife), was consistently improving, taking us to a new level. I felt firmly in control and pleased with the direction in our lives. I believe God had also provided visions of service that we were expected to carry out in both this and coming years. Three months later I was surprised with a diagnosis of a rare form of cancer. My life certainly turned on a dime. All was no longer well and surely beyond my personal control. Is this circumstance somehow related to the dream of 35 years ago? I do not know. I surely have experienced a diagnosis far more critical than a broken leg. Is there a need to plunge the knife deeper? Is God helping to do that for me? I am certain the knife will again be withdrawn and I will find myself closer to God. He is surely the only one in control.

Marilyn and I recently experienced our 31st anniversary. On her card I expressed a prayer that God will be good enough to grant us another 31 years together. I know He heard the prayer and I am sure He expects me to fulfill the visions given to me in January. I impatiently look forward to the day the knife is fully withdrawn and I am healthy once again and able and willing to fulfill His visions for our lives.

Richard A. Crousey 2007

THE TOUCH

As a very young child, my family attended a Presbyterian church. Located in a western Pennsylvania steel town, it was constructed of stone appropriately darkened by both age and the "by-products" of the mill. Mom had been raised in this church. Each week our parents dutifully accompanied my sister and I to Sunday School where my grandfather held the position of Superintendent. The morning worship service was always well-ordered with a routine that rarely varied. Children in the service were expected to sit quietly and pay proper attention. The sanctuary was dark with stained glass windows providing no chance of seeing anything interesting on the outside. All of us sat together as a family. It seems regimented as I look back. Perhaps this was a sign of the times. WWII had just concluded and there were plenty of soldiers home from the war now regimenting their families. My father was one of them. He had fought as a Marine in the South Pacific. As a child this provoked little thought, but later in life it would garner my utmost respect and gratitude.

Amusements being few, I learned to count on my grandfather each week to provide "a candy" during the service. Normally, he would offer Life Savers and most of the time my favorite, butter-rum. One Sunday an event so incidental occurred that it may appear foolish to share. While sitting quietly with my sister, I felt a hand on the back of my neck. It was soothing and gentle and I enjoyed the fingers slowly caressing my hair. Then I had a curious thought. Whose hand was this? It couldn't be Dad's as he was sitting too close. This I found disturbing.

Perhaps it was my grandfather's hand, surely a welcomed gesture. On the other hand, could it be a stranger. That just wouldn't seem right. I did not want to move away, yet I "needed to see" for certain whose hand it was. As I turned ever so slightly, the hand pulled away. It was, after all, Grandpa's hand. Why did I move my head? Whose hand did I think it would be? Would a stranger do something like that? I had been deceived by my insecurity.

Why should I remember this moment? Hard to say, but it sticks in my mind like yesterday. My reason for sharing it follows.

Let time pass forward to my being a young man. Once again I found myself at a church event. Actually, it was an overnight youth retreat at a country club north of Pittsburgh. The speaker for the night was an Episcopalian priest, John Guest. I do not remember the evening's topic but I do remember the communion service that followed. God's spirit was surely there. The speaker suggested that each of us should find a place to be alone with God. Immediately, I walked outside. It was a warm, dark night and lights were few and far between. This was good, I could walk well out onto the golf course where no one else would be. It was a nice walk with the grass yet untouched by dew. I found myself at a spot with no lights, a great place to be alone with God. Here I fell to my knees under a tree and prayed. The comfort I experienced at the communion service revisited me. Then there was an interruption. Someone softly, tenderly spoke my name, "Rick." The voice came from immediately behind me, (near the back of my head). Who would have followed me this far out onto the golf course? How dare they interrupt this serene experience? I did not want to break with the moment but I "needed to see" who had called my name. Reluctantly, I turned my head expecting to see the source of the voice. Instead I saw no one. I looked more closely, but it was all open grass except for the tree over my head. This is strange. What did I hear? Without an answer I went back to my knees hoping to find myself back in the same reverie. Only a moment later I heard my name softly spoken again. This time I was startled and jumped to my feet. My head encountered a branch on the way up and this, in turn, frightened a flock of roosting birds. The birds were as startled as me and flew off making a raucous of their own. The commotion set my heart pounding. Not seeing anyone behind me, I fled automatically back to the club house.

Whose voice had softly spoken my name? Again I had flinched in an effort to determine the source of a blessing only to find the experience, the opportunity gone.

Whose hand had it been, a stranger's? No, it was my grandfather's. A stranger would never behave so intimately. Whose voice was it that broke in on this more recent intimacy? I think not a stranger's. I have relived this incident repeatedly. Why did I choose to turn? Why didn't I sit quietly and listen to the voice? Why didn't I have the courage, the good sense to say, "Here am I," and continue in the grace of that moment.

Many years have now passed. I suspect I was hoping to encounter similar opportunities, but none to date. The moment seems to have been unique onto itself. There are many stories of people who "needed to see" for themselves. Thomas was one. God, however, honors those who do not require this proof, even in peculiar circumstances. If presented the chance again, would I now have the faith to respond differently or would I still "need" just a glance over my shoulder?

Richard A. Crousey June 28, 2007

TURNING ON A DIME

How many times do you wake up absolutely determined to have a bad day? This may sound strange. Who would wish a bad day upon themselves? It does, however, happen. So much is about choices. Sometimes they are conscious choices we are aware of making. Other times they are unconscious choices. Some days begin without such a decision, but events early in the day drive us in a direction and we come to expect the rest of the day to follow suit, good or bad. Knowing this to be true, let me describe a day I expect to always remember. In fact, I will share two such days that stand as monuments in my mind.

My four children were still young, with the oldest perhaps in her middle school years. My wife, Marilyn, and I had been planning a special family event. The Billy Graham Crusade was in Pittsburgh. We had a full size conversion van that would accommodate our family as well as friends our children could invite. The day arrives. I don't remember the early morning specifics but things were not going smoothly. Do you remember how hard it can be to get six people all moving in the same direction at one time? Odds are I cut myself shaving that morning. You know the kind of day I'm talking about: the eggs burning, the kids fighting, the dog throwing up on the carpet. [I'm not saying any of these things happened this particular day, but they might have.] The children's friends arrived and we got loaded up. Pushing off from the dock, I was not in the best of moods. We heard on the radio about traffic problems in the city and as I expected, other drivers were not courteous. Suddenly I heard a loud crash from the back of the vehicle.

One of the children's friends broke the van's sliding window by closing it far too hard. I suspect the breaking glass was the last straw. I exploded on everyone. My intention was for this event to be a good Christian witness not only for our children, but their friends as well. My witness failed to measure up. I screamed at the kids about the window and then at my wife. I determined we would never be able to find parking close to Three Rivers Stadium and we would have to park so far away that the walk wouldn't be worth the effort. Marilyn, however, retained some composure. She disputed with me that we were continuing the trip and I could drop everyone off outside the stadium and determine later what I would do. This being before cell phones, I would still have to find them at the stadium to either join them or just pick them up for the ride home. Options were limited to me and I was angry and I wanted everyone to know it. I was going to have a bad day and no one better get in my way! We did manage to find a distant parking place on the North Side, near the Aviary. Everyone got out and started the trek to the stadium. I trailed well behind, muttering to myself the whole way.

Now, the day becomes peculiar. I am fully charged with fury as I arrive outside the stadium. I hadn't prayed or done anything useful and I did not have a good thought in my mind. I take my first step into the stadium and my entire demeanor changes. It was so sudden and so stark I had to recognize it. What just happened? As I look back on the experience I wish I had stopped, turned around and stepped outside again just to see what might have happened. In just a moment I was filled with peace, no longer angry at the world and no longer concerned about the van window. We all went in and found a seat. The service was wonderful, though I don't remember any details about it. The experience worth remembering was had upon entry. Never before had I experienced such a distinct turn around in my emotional state.

I truly do not know what happened but I will offer a potential explanation. Years later [1999] we had a small Billy Graham sponsored crusade in Latrobe. Marilyn and I made it a point to get involved. We attended planning meetings and met with many others involved. One particular subject always in the forefront of the preparations was prayer. Everything was bathed in prayer before and during the event. Years before, was it prayer that had so bathed Three Rivers Stadium? Was it prayer that brought the spiritual world to reside so strongly at that place and at that time? Was it prayer that would not allow me to enter with such animosity and caused a renewal in my heart?

Earlier, I mentioned that there were two events I want to share with you. On this second occasion, there were again plans in place for a good day. I was going to work the morning and then leave to meet my son, Caleb, for a canoe trip on the Youghiogheny River. Upon arriving at work it was obvious that things were coming apart at the seams. It was not the beginning of a bad day, more like a terrible day. Through the morning nothing improved. It was clear I would have to break my appointment with Caleb. Finally I called his office only to find he had already left to meet me. What a predicament. I had no business leaving work nor could I abandon the time planned with my son. Most irresponsibly, I pulled things together as best I could and walked out of the factory. My mind was spinning, still trying to deal with the day's problems. I went home, changed my clothes and met Caleb as planned. We drove the hour to the river and still my mind was not at peace. Part of the problem was a guilt complex I was now carrying for having dropped my responsibilities. Arriving at Confluence, we slipped the canoe into the Youghiogheny and paddled from shore. We hadn't gone far when a sweet, comforting peace enveloped me. It was a total shock, completely unexpected. I commented to my son that I had never so quickly moved from the apparition of a hellish state to heavenly calm. The anxiety was gone. The day was beautiful and the water level good. We basked in the sun and swept through the cooling shade. We stopped for lunch and a swim and moved back out onto the water. It was a wonderful day together. The day is burned into my mind due to its unique dichotomy, standing again as a monument. I was timid about going to work the next morning, dreading what I may find. No need, it seems the place didn't even miss me. Oddly, I thought I was crucial in solving the problems of yesterday only to find them resolved without me.

What caused this to happen? Where there spiritual forces at work? Was there an unrecognized force trying to drag me down? Was there a more powerful force that lifted me up? Have you experienced moments like these that turn on a dime? Maybe there would be more of these peace filled moments if we allowed our spirit to trump the selfish demands of our soul.

Richard A. Crousey
July 11, 2009

THOUGHTFUL MOMENTS
ON THE ROAD

Morning in Michigan:

While traveling as a youth, I was faced with hours of boredom and much time to think. It simply goes with the territory. Things can be exciting or busy one moment followed by periods of slow times. There was always something to do like finding a place for the night and then you could sit quietly and experience the world around at a slower pace.

One memorable occasion occurred in Michigan. Having found a beautiful aspen glen to sleep in, a quick look about showed there was a small pond nearby. It always amazed me that there were so many places adjacent to roads or highways that provided both shelter and the intimacy of being much further from civilization than you actually were. After a good night's sleep I awoke with a fresh look at "my" pond. It had a sandy bottom rather than mud. This provided several opportunities not always available. One, sand is an excellent soap for cleaning up; a little coarse/harsh maybe but effective. Secondly, you could go in and out without getting feet muddy which further meant the possibility of easy swimming. It was a warm September morning with the sun shining brightly. Additional inspection showed the pond to have clear water with both a good in-flow and out-flow. After a fresh drink of cold water and following my bath it was time for a swim. The water was more than deep enough for swimming and with red-wing blackbirds and willows and aspens as my witnesses I found myself backstroking with my eyes to the sun and trees directly overhead. It was wonderful. After getting out and getting dressed I took a moment to think. In my life I was not likely to ever have the money to afford my own pond especially with the seclusion that came with this one; a pool perhaps with chemicals and all the expenses and work that go with it. This, however, required no work on my part nor did I have to own any land. This pond was here by God's hand and for the moment just for me.

Time Please:

Another occasion of note occurred somewhere in the southwest. I awoke one morning near a roadside and got up to ready myself for another day of hitch-hiking. Something was different this morning. What was it? Seemed like very few cars on the road. Was this Saturday? Was it Sunday? It finally dawned on me that I had no idea what day of the week it was. I was flushed with horror. How could I not know what day of the week it was? How far out of touch could I be? Then it occurred to me that under the circumstances it did not matter what day of the week it was. Now my emotions ran in the opposite direction to a sense of freedom from time I had never known. I suspect most of the world lives with the latter most of their lives, surely all primitive cultures do. Time is needed for things like science and maintaining schedules but not for much more; an anchor to life. Considering we are intended to be eternal beings, how strange we find time such a constraint and treat it like such a necessity.

Night in Manitoba:

It was September and weather should not be a problem for another month. Plans were to go from Sault Saint Marie to Vancouver. I quickly learned that upper Great Lake's weather was not similar to Pittsburgh's. At the "Sault" shelter was found as we (traveling with my good friend, Jim), imposed on some fellows moving into their dorm for the school year. Later we woke up with snow on the ground around us in Thunder Bay, trying to decide if it was better to freeze to death in sleeping bags or get up and get dressed first? Next stop was Winnipeg with the country flat and cold winds blowing hard. Enough of this, it's time to head south to North Dakota and alter our destination to Seattle. Somewhere south of Winnipeg it grew dark. Cars were traveling these flat straight roads at 100 mph with no chance of a hitch-hiker getting a ride. Now how do we sleep without freezing? Back off the road were hay bales. Here was our answer, to build a small one man enclosure out of hay bales with the last bale positioned about so it could be pulled over head and seclude us from the weather outside. It worked. It was a wonderful, refreshing sleep. Thank God for those hay bales. We needed that restful sleep as we awoke to cold hard winds still blowing in the morning.

Almost Like Never Having Been There:

Many time in my travels I traveled alone. There were some advantages. There were some disadvantages. The advantages were fairly obvious; no one to consult with; eat where you want; sleep where you want; etc. The negative aspect of this freedom was no one to share the experience with. You find yourself enamored by a view but with no one to share it with you find the experienced down-graded. Perhaps worst of all, years later you try sharing the experience with others to find you have forgotten much or most of it. Having a partner provides the triggers necessary to bring the view back into better focus.

WHO IS THE ENEMY?

Children see flowers blooming, dogs to walk, black berries to pick;
There are no enemies.

Youth are cruel, excluding some, making fun;
Is this an enemy?

Baseballs trade for camouflage, spirits reach for pride and glory;
Show me the enemy?

Walking through a misty morn, shots ring out, then a volley;
There is the enemy.

Not here before, we lay on our stomachs fearful, trembling;
Where is the enemy?

Fleeing quietly away we'll meet again;
Just a ghost, the enemy.

Another day, another dawn, boredom strikes through sultry heat;
Still no enemy.

Just a bend, small turn in the road; yards away, faces clear;
This is the enemy.

Scattered shots, muffled cries; mist gives way to sulfur smoke;
    Cries from the enemy.

Face to face we stare, then fall, heaving chests in mud & blood;
    He is the enemy?

Looks like me, has walked a dog; no glory here I see;
    The enemy is me.

A cross around his neck, his red, mine white;
    We're not enemies.

We find relief in each other's arms; he has my sister's hair;
    We close our eyes in brother's arms;
    This is no enemy.

We walk our dogs together now, the smell of sulfur gone.
    Friends forever, enemies never

Our home the same, our Savior one
    Thank God, no enemies!

Richard A. Crousey August, 25, 2009

WHO'S THE AUDIENCE?

Anyone who has spoken to an assembly of people knows the most important element is making sure the audience understands you. You must speak to those who are listening. You can use a vocabulary that will work for some but be inappropriate for others. You may refer to farming examples for some while for others literary examples are more apropos.

I remember an occasion when Marilyn and I were visiting some churches to see where we would like to attend. The closest church to our new home was pleasantly small and seemed a possibility. We attended one week and on the way home I asked Lyn what she thought about the service. She went on to say how much she enjoyed the service and the sermon. I was a bit surprised and cautioned Lyn about being her normal, overly kind self. Then I went on to say we would not likely go back there again. Naturally, she wanted to know what I found wrong with our visit. I "patiently" explained how the pastor was unable to speak the King's English and made numerous grammatical, pronunciation and vocabulary errors. It was so bad that I couldn't hear what he was trying to say as I regularly tripped over his errors. Lyn found this unusual and said she easily understood his message. Then (as she commonly would) cut me down like a big oak tree, "Seems to me the problem may be more yours than his." Ouch, how do you respond to that? Was my critical spirit the major issue here? Was it really my problem? Truthfully, it didn't matter who was at fault. Was he speaking specifically to me or reaching out to the rest of the congregation? If he was reaching out to the rest of the congregation, perhaps he had been successful and I was out of place with my comment. (Perhaps too this was the wrong congregation for us.) The next week we did go again and I tried to struggle past the mistakes to glean the meaning of the sermon. It was painful but I was able to do better. Each week got progressively better. The pastor was not changing but I was adapting to the circumstances and trying to listen to the meaning of his messages as Marilyn had eloquently suggested. We've now been going to this church for 30 years. Our first pastor never did change and probably couldn't if he tried. He lacked the education to get past my first criticisms but I had learned to listen with different ears. He really had a lot to say to those willing to listen.

I have now been teaching a men's Sunday school class for years, constantly trying to engage the class and teach what God has been sharing with me. We surely do have a good time, though few in number, and there are those wonderful times when I am really able to connect well with the class. Unfortunately, there are also those times when all seems to fall on deaf ears. Oddly, enough this deafness does not relate to how well prepared I have been to teach. Sometimes this is so but other times it even appears the opposite may be true. On good days I am frequently surprised by the words coming from my mouth...thoughts I don't even remember considering before. So I have learned to be a good listener while I speak. I don't mean this to sound haughty. It just seems the Holy Spirit takes control on those really good days and how rewarding that can be.

With this background, our present pastor occasionally asks me to teach the Wednesday night service. The same issues apply but the audience is surely different for me and I try to handle the service accordingly. Women are far more willing to speak whether men are around or not. Men, however, tend to be quiet, even non-responsive when women are around (therefore, the Men's Sunday School class).

So allow me to share the events from one of these Wednesday evening services. The week previous I was given a lot of insight and although it took a long time to prepare, everything had fallen together in a really interesting way. It was not a traditional message. Maybe that's why I was so excited about presenting it. Near the beginning of the service a man came in who rarely attended the services and he sat way back in the last row. I didn't know where he lived, just that he sometimes came with others I did not recognize. Rich was suffering from throat/tongue cancer and this made him very hard to understand and this time he came alone. My big moment had come and now it was time to walk down this well-prepared, creative path. Plod would have been a better word than walk as things were moving slowly at best. You must understand that I do not preach regardless of the forum. The only thing I know how to do is teach. As I teach I always reach out for audience participation. So plodding along is not a good thing. This class required a great deal of class participation and no one seemed as excited as I was. We were speaking about taking a Mediterranean cruise. At first everyone was interested in doing this. As we slowly moved on and the comfort level of the cruise changed, less people remained interested in the voyage. Finally, it became clear we were talking about being crew members on an ancient commercial vessel, circa 30 AD. The further along we went there was only one person who remained interested all of the way until the end…it was Rich. Each time I asked for a volunteer for the changing conditions his hand was first up. We ended up talking about being willing to cast out well past the vision of shore so the ship could be more profitable. Before sextants, this was risky business and required faith both in oneself and being certain of the captain's ability to read the stars and get us safely in port again. Believe me, everyone seemed to lose interest early on except for Rich. By the end of the lesson I had expected everybody to withdraw willingly from the crew but not Rich. He was absolutely enthusiastic in the way he continued to raise his hand.

The lesson parallel was about our willingness to go beyond our natural limitations and fears, to step out in faith in service for our King. Willing to trust our Captain Jesus with our very lives knowing as we faithfully serve him He will bring us safely to shore.

The lesson had not gone well, despite all my efforts. People lacked not just the faith to get onboard our vessel but they had no interest in even making the trip. I had hoped to get back to speak with Rich but found he left as surreptitiously as he had arrived. I was curious as to what he had been thinking. I was also concerned that if I engaged him perhaps I would not understand what he was saying. OK, time to rap things up, lick my wounds and go home.

Weeks later I overheard a conversation. Something caught my ear and it sounded like they may have been talking about Rich. Butting in, I asked further about their conversation. It seemed Rich had died. On further inquiry it seems he died only a couple of days following our service. I was seriously saddened and chastised myself about not making a greater effort to know and understand this man. Nothing more came to mind. Then a couple of days later I sensed the Lord trying to get through to me. This was the first time I could tie the lesson together with the man. My audience had never been the regular Wednesday night church body. It had been Rich from the beginning and I was too thick to pick up on it. Rich knew he was about to take a journey of faith through unfamiliar seas. He was more than willing to place his faith in the Captain and happy to know he would be directed safely into port.[1] I truly hope the lesson helped him. One thing I know for sure…Rich was my audience.

[1] "…his disciples started across the lake with him in the boat…Suddenly a windstorm struck the lake. Waves started splashing into the boat, and it was about to sink. Jesus was in the back of the boat with his head on a pillow, and he was asleep. His disciples woke him and said, "Teacher, don't you care that we're about to drown?" Jesus got up and ordered the wind and the waves to be quiet. The wind stopped, and everything was calm. Jesus asked is disciples, "Why were you afraid? Don't you have any faith?"

Mark 4: 35-40 CEV

Richard Crousey April, 2009

# THE FINAL CHAPTER

IN MEMORY OF THE
LOVE OF MY LIFE

Richard Alan Crousey
November 28, 1948 - February 9, 2010

"Now we see through the glass darkly,
but then face to face."
I Corinthians 13:12

When I see a river just right to canoe, or hear 'Come Thou Fount' my
    thoughts race to you
We shared our home for 34 years, filled with laughter, joy and tears
Raised four great kids to serve our God: Cambric, Caleb, Josh and Rod
In everything they say and do, each of our 4 kids [and 11 grandkids]
    remind me of you
Latrobe Steele was your second home, often working dawn to dusk,
No matter what you had to do, you always came home to us
As supervising engineer, you really loved your 'Furnace Crew', And all
    the special relationships and friendships that you knew
God burdened your heart with love to teach, so many lives you tried
    to reach
In Sunday School at Tree of Life or just one soul in need
Your life and being just may be the only Bible some would read

It's been two years since you left our earthly home, God carried you in
love to His heavenly throne
No more fear, cancer or pain - your work on earth is done, yet your
touch on our lives has just begun.
We all miss you - your wife and children, your sister and Mom
Yes, all your friends and family, and yet we rejoice that you are 'home'
Where we will see you again

Marilyn Crousey, February 9, 2012

OUR DAD

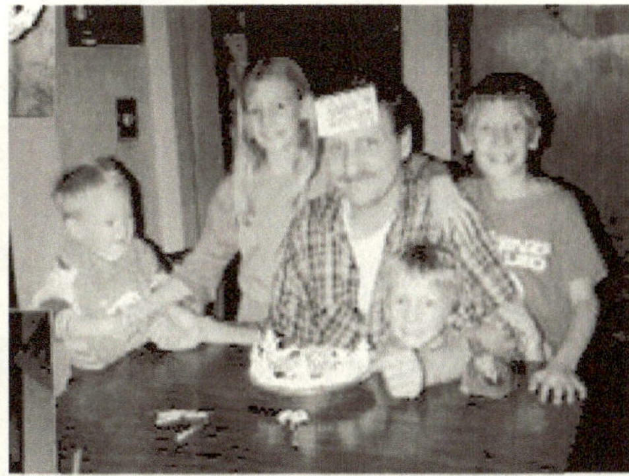

Our dad. A man who feared God above anyone or anything else, which meant not allowing the trivial opinions of the world cloud his view of reality. Life was not about reaching self-proclaimed goals, but instead cherishing each moment granted us because life is truly "made" of those gifts. Whether it was a walk through the woods, an intense baseball game or sitting in a church pew; by pausing "under a hemlock" we recognize that moment as a fleeting gift from God. Now, though this collection of his short stories, you are also able to glance through a window of Dad's heart. May you be blessed as we are and remember to hold dear to the "small," passing moments.

RICK CROUSEY

The Younger Years

Today my brother stopped by. He has terminal cancer and none of us are fooled by the gravity of his situation. Rick gave me a long, strong hug and I was reminded again that he is a 'bag of bones'. I detected a fever but said nothing about it. Instead I rambled on and on about something silly. I sense he is departing very soon and I am profoundly sad.

It is 3 am and sleep totally escapes me and so I am thinking non-stop about my brother. First thought/word that comes to mind is *pensive*. Rick is a professional thinker about pretty much everything. Lucky for me! As youngsters, I let him do the thinking and worrying for us both – that left me carefree.

Second word that comes to mind is *non-conformist*. Listen to Henry Nilsson's 'The Point' CD. Rick will approve and you will have great discussions about little Oblio. Final word to describe him is *idealist*. Don't you agree?

Karen (Crousey) Tribou November, 2009

TO THE MEMORY OF
DICK CROUSEY

FROM HIS FRIENDS AND CO-WORKERS:
The Furnace Crew –
Larry, Bill, Joe and John

It was a sad day for all when word came that Dick had passed away. With heavy hearts we think back and reflect on days gone by when we, as a group, worked on Special Projects with Dick.

We all have some special story to tell about our friend and boss, but we all agree on one thing – Dick was a very special boss to us as well as a friend. When things needed to be done, Dick got that task given to him.

He took great pride in the challenge put forth to him to get the job accomplished. Not just completed, but better that it was before. He loved new ideas and especially when they came from us. It brought a smile to his face that we cared about what we were working on as much as he did. Dick was a hands-on supervisor and worked right beside us. He treated us with great respect and cared deeply for us and our needs and concerns, whatever they might be.

When Dick would go on vacation, he would lay out our projects for us and always made sure materials were at hand for each job. Usually we would run into a snag here and there, so we had to wait for Dick to return to solve them. I remember once, on his return from vacation, guys were lined up and down the hall in front of his office waiting their turn to speak to him on some issue of their job. He would smile, give a little laugh, and say "What do you need?" Dick was a problem solver with a great upbeat tempo that rubbed off on all of us.

He was a deeply religious person and used this faith in God to carry us all through our daily tasks. We felt the strength that exuded from his faith in God. He was a beacon of light to us. To have Dick no longer with us is like not having the sun. Dick, to say we miss you is an understatement and words cannot describe how deeply we felt for you as our friend and supervisor. May God carry you on your journey with great care. God bless you for your short time with us. You will be forever in our hearts.

God bless!
Larry, Bill, Joe and John

I hope enjoy this copy of <u>The Stuff of Monuments</u>. Richard composed many of these short stories during our most difficult time. He chose to use his four hour chemo treatments as an opportunity to share what God placed on his heart. I pray that you find encouragement, hope and the love of Jesus within its pages.

God Bless You
Marilyn D Crousey
<u>mcrousey@gmail.com</u>

Donations may be made to the
Richard A Crousey Legacy Fund at the
Community Foundation of Westmoreland County
<u>cfwestmoreland.org</u> or the
Richard A Crousey Memorial Fund at
Tree of Life Assembly of God
1005 Cedar Street, Latrobe, PA 15650